Grade 3

SSPP School

Donated by The Toledo family

The Mystery of the Blind Writer

by Kal Gezi and Ann Bradford
illustrated by Mina Gow McLean

CHILDRENS PRESS, CHICAGO

Distributed by Childrens Press, 1224 West Van Buren Street, Chicago, Illinois 60607.

Library of Congress Cataloging in Publication Data

Gezi, Kalil I
 The mystery of the blind writer.

 (The Maple Street five)
 SUMMARY: When a tape recorder is stolen from a blind writer, five children help him search for the thief.
 [1. Blind—Fiction.   2. Physically handicapped—Fiction.   3. Mystery and detective stories]
I. Bradford, Ann, joint author.   II. McLean, Mina Gow.   III. Title.
PZ7.G33902Mu   [E]   80-12395
ISBN 0-89565-145-9

Maria,   Barry,   Tom,   Vern,   and Linda

PRINCIPAL

stood waiting in the principal's office. They
were there to welcome a guest.

"How will he get here?" asked Maria.

"He'll walk," said the principal, Mr. Johnson. "He lives about six blocks away."

"Walk?" said Barry. "When he can't see?"

"He has learned how to get around, even though he can't see," said Mr. Johnson. "And he has a very good guide dog to help him."

"Here he comes now," said Tom.

"Oh, what a beautiful dog!" said Barry. "It's a German shepherd!"

The five children and the principal went out to greet the blind man, Mr. Rubin. Mr. Rubin had come to speak to the first, second, and third grades. He was going to tell about his job. He was a writer.

Maria, Barry, Tom, Vern, and Linda talked to Mr. Rubin. Then they led him to the classroom. All the other children were there, waiting.

"Good morning, Mr. Rubin," said Mrs. Lopez. "Welcome to the Kennedy school."

Soon Mr. Rubin was speaking. He told the children about his work. He had been many places and written about many, many things.

"I'd like to turn on my tape recorder," he said. "I'll want you to ask me questions soon. I may use some of your questions in my writing."

Soon Mr. Rubin's speech was over. Then he said, "Now, any questions? Please ask me anything you want to know."

There were a few moments of silence. Then Vern raised his hand.

"Yes, Vern," said Mrs. Lopez.

"How do you get around?" asked Vern.

"I have worked to strengthen my sense of direction," said Mr. Rubin. "I know when I turn left. I know when I turn right. My guide dog, Bingo, helps me when I am outside. He helps me cross streets. He makes sure I know about steps. He makes sure I don't bump into things. Bingo is very important to me. Here, let me show you."

At a word, Bingo was at Mr. Rubin's side. Mr. Rubin took the leash. He and Bingo began walking. They were headed right toward a wall. But Bingo turned before they got to the wall. Mr. Rubin turned too. Bingo turned to avoid a table. Mr. Rubin turned too. In this way, the dog and man walked all around the room.

"You see," said Mr. Rubin. "With Bingo, I could walk anywhere!"

"How did you know where our school is?" someone else asked.

"When we first moved in, my wife helped me. We walked all over the neighborhood. I've walked by your school many times."

"Mr. Rubin," said Linda, "how did you become a writer?"

Mr. Rubin laughed and said, "I applied for many jobs. But no one was willing to hire a blind person. At least not for the kinds of jobs I wanted. So, I decided to write books."

"But, if you can't see," said Tom, "how do you write? Don't the words end up on top of each other?"

Again Mr. Rubin laughed. "Sometimes they do," he said. "So I found an easier way. I speak what I want to write into this tape recorder. Later, my wife types the words."

"How do you recognize people?" Maria asked.

"Oh, it isn't too hard," said Mr. Rubin. "Let me show you."

He asked for five children wearing rings on their fingers to step forward. Five children did. He shook hands with each of them. Each told his or her name. He asked them to stand in a different order. Then, touching each hand, he told that person the right name.

"Wow! How can you tell?" asked the children.

"By the shapes of your rings and the feel of your hands," said Mr. Rubin.

The writer then asked the children to shut their eyes. After a moment, he said, "Now you can open your eyes." The children did.

"Are each of you the same person now as when your eyes were shut?" he asked.

"Yes," answered the children.

"And I'm the same person now as when I could see," said Mr. Rubin. "We blind people do not want you to pity us. Just treat us as you treat other people."

All the students came up to the writer. They talked and talked to him. Some shook his hand and told their names. He remembered every name! Some bent to pet his guide dog, Bingo.

The teacher thanked Mr. Rubin, who left soon with his tape recorder. Bingo walked along beside him. The children watched him through the window, until he was out of sight.

Later, Maria heard a funny sound at the window. She looked over. There was Bingo!

"Mrs. Lopez!" she shouted. "Bingo's back!"

"Oh, my," said Mrs. Lopez. "Please bring him in, Maria."

Maria opened the door and Bingo rushed in. His tail was wagging. His body was shaking. And Mr. Rubin was nowhere in sight. Bingo ran to the window and barked. Then he ran back to Maria, then back to the window again.

"You five children who welcomed Mr. Rubin," said the teacher, "go with Bingo. I'll call Mr. Johnson. He'll meet you at the front door of the school. See if you can find Mr. Rubin."

Bingo led the five children and principal to a grassy plaza. A large fountain was in the center. Bingo sniffed all around the fountain. Mr. Rubin was not there.

"What could have happened to him?" Barry asked.

"Maybe he was kidnapped!" Tom answered.

"Perhaps he was hit by a car," said Linda.

"Let's not get too worried," said Mr. Johnson. "We'll go back to the school and call the police. Perhaps they can help us find Mr. Rubin."

19

Soon the children were back at the school. They petted Bingo while the principal went to call the police. When he came back, he was smiling.

"Mr. Rubin is O.K.," he said. "He's at the police station. Someone grabbed his tape recorder away from him and then ran. Mr. Rubin told Bingo to chase the thief. That left Mr. Rubin standing all alone. Bingo didn't come back and didn't come back. Mr. Rubin began to worry. So he asked a lady to help him find the police station."

"I'll bet he's glad to know Bingo is here," said Barry.

"He certainly is! The police will bring him over to get Bingo."

Soon Mr. Rubin arrived. Bingo was so happy to see him! Mr. Rubin hugged and petted Bingo until Bingo calmed down.

"Well, now," said Mr. Rubin, "at least I have Bingo back. The police say they'll try to find the thief. But I couldn't tell them what he looked like. I don't think they'll have much success. I'll just have to save my money for a new tape recorder."

"I wish we could find the thief for you," said Maria.

"I doubt that you could," said Mr. Rubin. "But there is one way you could try. After school, could you children walk with me to where Bingo took you? Maybe we could find out something."

"O.K.," said the children.

"Call your parents," said Mrs. Lopez. "Make sure they don't mind. Tell them I'll be with you too."

After school, Bingo led the group to the grassy plaza.

"This is where the thief got the recorder," said Mr. Rubin.

Several people were in the plaza. "Let's ask around," said Linda. "Maybe someone saw the robbery."

So the children spread out. "Were you here earlier?" they asked people. "Did you see a man rob our friend?"

"No," said one woman. "I just got here."

"No," said a man.

Mr. Rubin sat down on a bench. Barry took Bingo's leash. He and the dog walked around to the other side of the fountain.

"Were you here earlier?" Barry asked an old man.

"Oh, yes," said the man. "Been playing checkers, with my friend. Say! That dog! I've seen him before! Isn't that the blind man's dog?"

"Yes!" said Barry. "Yes, he is!"

"Ahhh! Quite a bit of excitement that was! Some man grabbed something from the blind man. Then the thief took off running, this dog after him. You should have seen that man run! This dog chased him, down Cedar Street."

"Thank you!" said Barry. "That's what we wanted to find out." He and Bingo ran back to tell the others.

Soon all of them were walking down Cedar Street. Bingo sniffed and sniffed. They walked for two blocks. Then Bingo barked loudly and started up another street.

"We'd better follow Bingo," said Mr. Rubin. For three more blocks, the group followed Bingo.

All of a sudden, Bingo stopped. He growled.

A man had just come out of an apartment and was headed toward them. He carried a brown bag. He saw the dog and started running. Bingo took off after him. With a great leap, Bingo knocked the man down.

"Oof!" grunted the man as he fell on the grass. The brown bag in his hand tore open.

Maria got there first. "Look!" she shouted. She grabbed the bag. Inside was a tape recorder.

"Mr. Rubin," she called, running toward the writer. "Is this your tape recorder?"

Mr. Rubin touched the recorder, felt around it. "Yes, it is," he said. "Feel these bumps on the bottom? They stand for 'R' in Braille!"

Mrs. Lopez and the children surrounded the man. He was still sitting on the grass. Bingo growled and stood guard over him.

"Shouldn't have tried to sell it so soon," the man muttered. "Should have kept it hidden!"

"You shouldn't have stolen it in the first place," said Tom.

"Who asked you?" grumbled the thief.

A crowd was gathering. Someone ran to call the police. In no time at all, a police car was there. A police woman came over. When she heard the story, she arrested the man.

As the police car drove away, Mr. Rubin thanked everyone. He shook hands with Mrs. Lopez. He shook hands with each child.

"Come to see me Saturday," he said. "We'll celebrate!"

So, on Saturday, all five children went to see Mr. Rubin. The children had such fun! They played with Bingo. They ate the hot dogs Mrs. Rubin fixed for them.

Then, Mr. Rubin signed copies of his latest book, *Children Are Heroes!* And he gave a copy to each child.

"I didn't know you five when I wrote this book," he said. "But you certainly are heroes!"